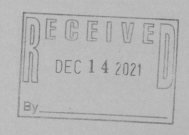

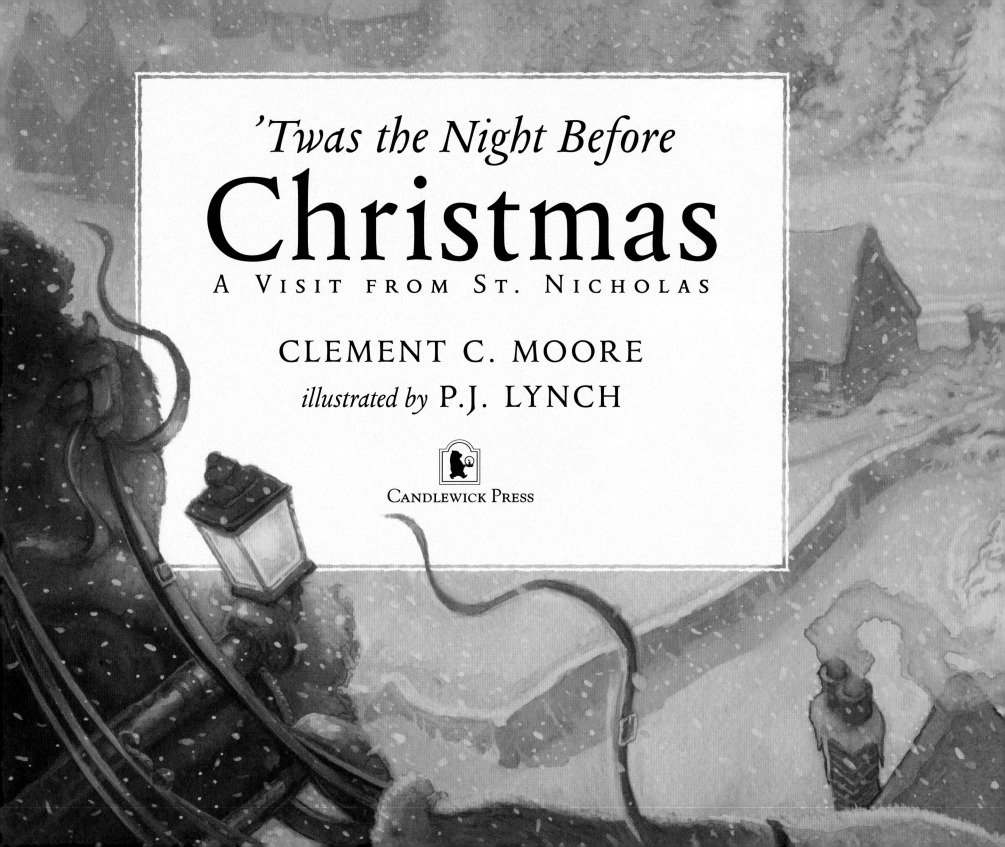

'Twas the Night Before
Christmas
A Visit from St. Nicholas

CLEMENT C. MOORE
illustrated by P.J. LYNCH

CANDLEWICK PRESS

'TWAS THE NIGHT

BEFORE CHRISTMAS

'Twas the night before Christmas,
when all through the house
Not a creature was stirring,
not even a mouse;

The stockings were hung
by the chimney with care,
In hopes that St. Nicholas
soon would be there;

The children were nestled
    all snug in their beds;
While visions of sugar-plums
    danced in their heads;
And mamma in her 'kerchief,
    and I in my cap,
Had just settled our brains
    for a long winter's nap,

When out on the lawn
   there arose such a clatter,
I sprang from my bed
   to see what was the matter.
Away to the window
   I flew like a flash,
Tore open the shutters
   and threw up the sash.

The moon on the breast
of the new-fallen snow,
Gave a lustre of midday
to objects below,
When what to my wondering
eyes did appear,
But a miniature sleigh
and eight tiny rein-deer,
With a little old driver
so lively and quick,
I knew in a moment
he must be St. Nick.
More rapid than eagles
his coursers they came,
And he whistled, and shouted,
and called them by name:

"Now, *Dasher!* now, *Dancer!*
    now *Prancer* and *Vixen!*
On, *Comet!* on, *Cupid!*
    on, *Donner* and *Blitzen!*
To the top of the porch!
    to the top of the wall!
Now dash away! dash away!
    dash away all!"

As leaves that before
the wild hurricane fly,
When they meet with an obstacle,
mount to the sky;
So up to the housetop
the coursers they flew
With the sleigh full of toys,
and St. Nicholas too—

And then, in a twinkling,
I heard on the roof
The prancing and pawing
of each little hoof.

As I drew in my head,
   and was turning around,
Down the chimney St. Nicholas
   came with a bound.
He was dressed all in fur,
   from his head to his foot,
And his clothes were all tarnished
   with ashes and soot;
A bundle of toys
   he had flung on his back,
And he looked like a peddler
   just opening his pack.

His eyes—how they twinkled!
    his dimples, how merry!
His cheeks were like roses,
    his nose like a cherry!
His droll little mouth
    was drawn up like a bow,
And the beard on his chin
    was as white as the snow;
The stump of a pipe
    he held tight in his teeth,
And the smoke, it encircled
    his head like a wreath;

He had a broad face
    and a little round belly
That shook when he laughed,
    like a bowl full of jelly.
He was chubby and plump,
    a right jolly old elf,
And I laughed when I saw him,
    in spite of myself;
A wink of his eye
    and a twist of his head
Soon gave me to know
    I had nothing to dread;
He spoke not a word,
    but went straight to his work,
And filled all the stockings;
    then turned with a jerk,

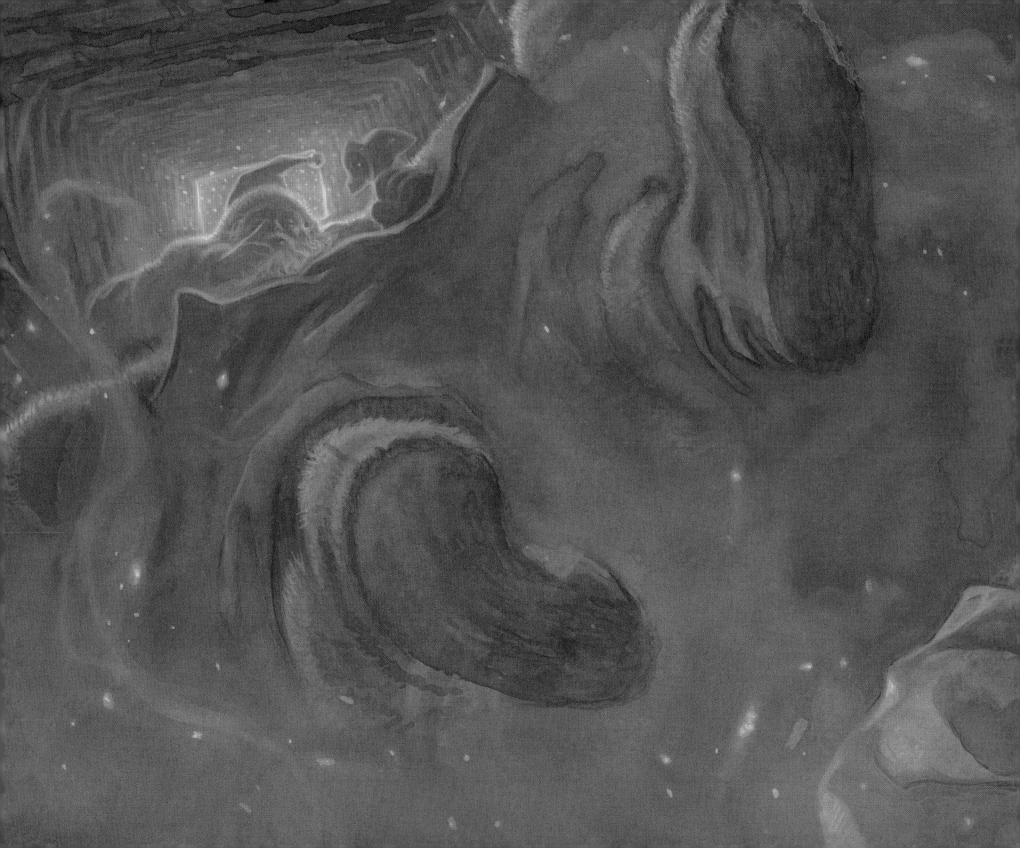

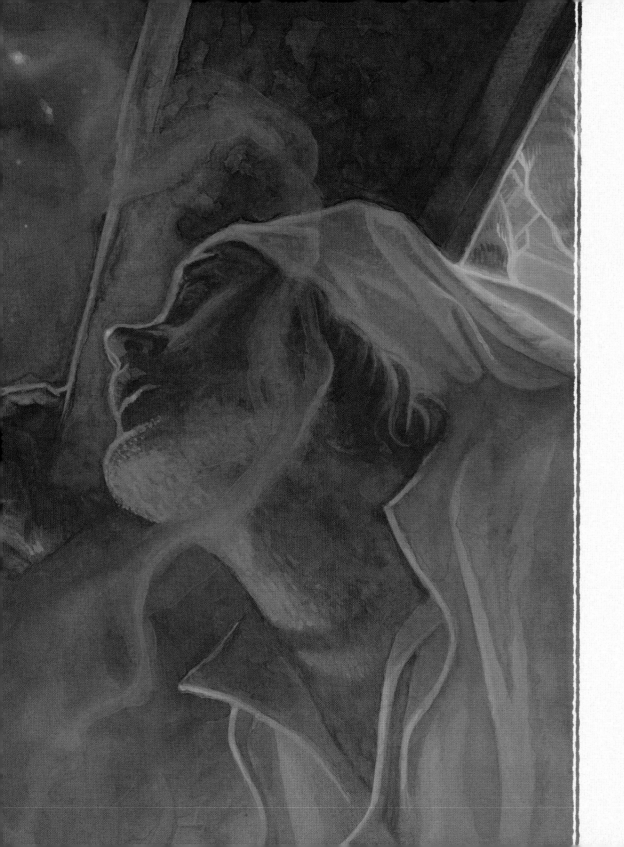

And laying his finger
   aside of his nose,
And giving a nod,
   up the chimney he rose;

He sprang to his sleigh,
    to his team gave a whistle,
And away they all flew
    like the down of a thistle.
But I heard him exclaim,
    ere he drove out of sight—

"Happy Christmas to all,
    and to all a good night!"

For Bruno and Flora, and for Oisín, Jacq, Scott, and Eimhinn

With special thanks to Ben Norland and Denise Johnstone-Burt